THE SECRET GARDEN

THE SECRET GARDEN

FRANCES HODGSON BURNETT

Retold by
Louise Betts

Illustrated by
Karen Pritchett

Troll Associates

Library of Congress Cataloging in Publication Data

Betts, Louise.
    The secret garden.

    Summary: Ten-year-old Mary comes to live in a
lonely house on the Yorkshire moors and discovers an
invalid cousin and the mysteries of a locked garden.
    [1. Orphans—Fiction.   2. Gardens—Fiction.
3. Physically handicapped—Fiction.   4. Yorkshire—
Fiction]   I. Pritchett, Karen, 1952-   , ill.
II. Burnett, Frances Hodgson, 1849-1924. Secret
Garden.   III. Title.
PZ7.B934Se   1988   [Fic]   87-15490
ISBN 0-8167-1203-4 (lib. bdg.)
ISBN 0-8167-1204-2 (pbk.)

early everyone agreed Mary Lennox
was a most disagreeable child. She wore a sour expression
on her face. And her face, like her hair and body, was thin.
She appeared frail and ill. And much of the time, she was.

Mary lived in a big house in India. Although she was an
only child, she hardly ever saw her parents. Her father was
always too busy to play with Mary. Her mother, who was
admired for her great beauty, cared only for parties and
fun—not for her little daughter.

Mary's mother had not wanted a daughter at all. So when
Mary was born, her mother hired a nanny to take care of
her. The nanny's job was to keep Mary as quiet as possible
and out of sight. Mary was a sickly, complaining baby.

In time, she grew up to become a sickly, complaining young girl, who was completely used to having her own way. Her nanny and the servants gave in to Mary so that she would not cry and disturb her mother. It was obvious to all that Mary was a selfish, spoiled little girl.

Mary's life stayed the same until she was ten years old. Then, without warning, a terrible disease swept through India. Many people died. Even servants at Mary's house began to die from the disease.

One very hot morning, Mary awoke with a strange feeling. She could hear people outside moaning and wailing and running around. Mary was afraid and called to her nanny. No one came. As the sounds outside grew louder, Mary grew more frightened. She hid in the nursery all day. She had to eat biscuits and fruit left from the day before. Most of the time, Mary cried. Soon she had cried herself to sleep.

When Mary awoke the following morning, everything was silent. She felt alone, but she also felt angry that everyone had forgotten about her. Suddenly, the door opened and two soldiers came in. They were surprised to find Mary there.

"Why did nobody come?" Mary demanded, stamping her foot.

"Poor little kid!" said one of the men. "There's nobody *left* to come."

That was how Mary learned that her parents had died from the terrible disease. Most of the servants had also died, while the rest had run away. With no one left in India to look after her, Mary was put on a ship and sent to live with her uncle. His name was Archibald Craven, and he lived at Misselthwaite Manor in Yorkshire, England.

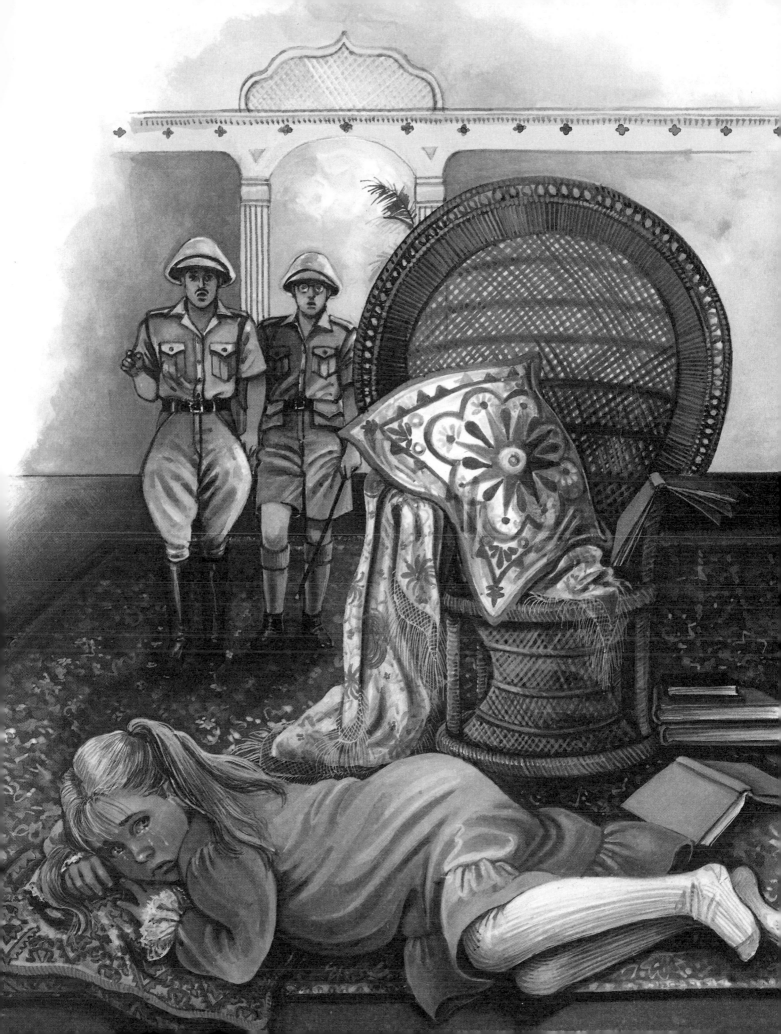

When Mary arrived in London, she was met by her uncle's housekeeper, Mrs. Medlock. She was a stout woman with very red cheeks and sharp black eyes. The housekeeper thought Mary was a spoiled child. Mary thought Mrs. Medlock was the most unpleasant person she had ever met. Mary often thought people were unpleasant, but of course she didn't know she was unpleasant herself.

On the train north to Yorkshire, Mrs. Medlock told Mary about Misselthwaite Manor. She said the house was big and gloomy. It had hundreds of rooms that were almost all closed up and locked. Around the house was a big park, and beyond that was the moor.

"What's the moor like?" asked Mary.

"It's just miles and miles of dreary, bare land. Nothing grows on it but wildflowers and shrubs, and nothing lives there but wild ponies and sheep," said Mrs. Medlock.

The two were quiet for a while. Then, in the carriage ride to Misselthwaite Manor, Mrs. Medlock said, "Don't expect to see your uncle. He never troubles himself about anyone. He's got a crooked back and was always a bitter person until he got married. His wife was sweet and pretty, and he adored her. But when she died, it made him stranger than ever. He's away from home most of the time, so you must look after yourself."

When they arrived, Misselthwaite Manor was dark, except for one dim light. A butler opened a huge oak door and told Mrs. Medlock, "You're to take her to her room. Mr. Craven is going to London in the morning and won't see her now."

Mary was led upstairs and down many long hallways to a room with a fire in it. Supper was on the table.

"Here," said Mrs. Medlock. "You'll live in this room and the next. Just see that you stay here. I don't want you poking about the rest of the house."

On this first night at Misselthwaite Manor, Mary had never felt quite so sad in all her life.

The next morning, Mary was awakened by a young housemaid. She was raking the ashes from the bedroom fireplace. Her name was Martha. She smiled and chatted as she worked. Mary thought it was odd that a servant would speak so freely to her. In India, Mary had slapped her nanny's face once in anger. Somehow, Mary knew she could not treat Martha that way.

As the girl talked on in her good-natured way, Mary gradually began to listen. Martha was describing her eleven brothers and sisters who lived in a little cottage on the moor. "It's hard for my mother to feed them all. But the fresh air on the moor makes them strong and healthy. My brother Dickon, who's twelve, is always out on the moor. He's a kind lad and animals like him. Why, he's even tamed a wild pony!"

Mary was impressed with anyone who could tame a wild pony. She thought about that while picking at her breakfast. Martha thought Mary was wasteful not to eat it all, but Mary never did have much of an appetite. After Martha finished cleaning, she showed Mary the way outside.

"Go out and look at the gardens," Martha suggested.

"There's not much there now, but they'll be beautiful in summer." She thought a moment, then added, "One of the gardens has been locked up. No one's been in it for ten years."

"Why?" asked Mary.

"Mr. Craven had it shut after his wife died so suddenly," said Martha. "It was her garden, but now he hates it. He locked the door, dug a hole, and buried the key."

Mary idly strolled through the grounds of Misselthwaite Manor. They were huge, divided by high brick walls surrounding gardens that looked bare and wintry. Green doors led from one garden to the next. Suddenly, an old man with a large spade over his shoulder walked into the vegetable garden where Mary was standing. He seemed startled to see Mary and stared at her with his grouchy, old face. Mary looked coldly back at him.

"Can I look at the other gardens?" Mary asked.

"If you like. But there's nothing to see," said the man.

Mary shrugged and walked from garden to garden through the green doors. She hoped to find a door that wouldn't open, for that would be the mysterious garden.

Finally, she came to an orchard that was also surrounded by a wall—but there was no door anywhere. Behind the wall Mary could see the tops of trees and a robin perched on one of the highest branches. The bird was singing a song, and its cheerful whistle gave Mary a pleasant feeling. She listened until the robin flew away.

Mary found the old man digging in the vegetable garden. "There was no door into one of the gardens," she said.

"Which garden?" the man asked gruffly.

"The one on the other side of that wall. I could see the treetops where a robin was singing."

To Mary's surprise, a smile spread over the old man's face. She had never realized how much nicer a person looked smiling. Then the gardener whistled, and the robin came flying over the wall. It landed near the man's foot.

"Here he is!" said the old man, as he watched the red-breasted bird hop about, pecking at the earth. "He always comes when I call him. Poor critter. You see, he got sick and was too weak to fly south with his family for the winter. So they had to leave him here. He's lonely. I'm lonely myself, except when he's with me."

"I'm lonely too," said Mary. "I've never had any friends."

"We're probably a good bit alike then, you and me," said the old man. "We're as sour as we seem." He then introduced himself as Ben Weatherstaff, the gardener of Misselthwaite Manor.

Mary told him who she was. She was still hurt from what he said about her. Mary had never heard the truth about herself. Now that she did, she did not like it. Her thoughts were interrupted by the robin's singing from an apple tree.

"He wants to be friends with you," said Ben.

Mary moved toward the bird and asked gently, "Will you be my friend?"

Her soft, kind voice surprised Ben. "Why, you said that like a real child."

Just then the robin flew away, over the wall beyond the orchard. "There must be a door to that garden," said Mary.

"None that anyone can find," said Ben. "And don't be nosy." He walked off without saying goodbye.

13

Mary spent most of her days outdoors. The fresh air and walking brought a healthy glow to her skin. At night, she liked to sit by the fireplace and talk with Martha.

"Why does Mr. Craven hate the garden?" Mary asked Martha one evening.

Martha answered in a quiet voice. "It was Mrs. Craven's garden, you see. She made it when they first got married. They were the only ones allowed in it. But one day, while Mrs. Craven was sitting on a tree branch, it snapped. She fell and was hurt so badly that the next day she died. Mr. Craven never recovered from the shock of her death. So he had the garden locked up. And no one's been in it since."

Outside, the wind howled. Mary thought she heard something else too. "Do you hear anyone crying?"

Martha looked surprised. "N-no," she said quickly. "It's the wind . . . or the cook. She's had a toothache all day."

Mary did not believe Martha. She felt Martha was hiding something from her. But what?

The following morning, it rained heavily. Both girls were huddled again by the fire, talking.

"On a day like this at home," said Martha, "we stay inside too. All of us but Dickon, that is. He goes out rain or shine. And he's always making new animal friends. Some he even brings home with him, like the fox cub and young crow he found." Martha spoke a little while longer about Dickon and the rest of her family, then left to do her chores.

With the rain still beating down outside, Mary decided to spend the morning exploring inside. Most of the doors to the manor's rooms were locked. But one was open. She entered a room full of curious furniture and ornaments. There were embroidered hangings on the wall. Inside a cabinet were little carved ivory elephants. Mary took them out and played with them on the carpet. She hardly noticed the tiny gray mice on the couch nearby.

On the way back to her room, Mary lost her way. Finally, she found her floor, but she was still some distance from her room when she heard a cry. It was a short, fretful, childish whine. She leaned against the wall to hear better.

"What are you doing here?" said an angry Mrs. Medlock, startling Mary. The housekeeper took Mary by the arm and pulled her away.

"I heard someone crying!" said Mary

"You heard nothing of the sort!" snapped Mrs. Medlock. She then dragged Mary down the hall and pushed her through the door of her room. "You stay where you're told," the woman hissed.

Mary sat on the rug. She was angry herself now. "There *was* someone crying!" she said. "And someday I'm going to find out who it was!"

Two days later, the storm ended. The sky was clear, and everything seemed fresh and lovely. It was Martha's day off, and the young maid was getting ready to cross the moor and visit her family.

"You'd like my mother," said Martha.

"I'd like her and Dickon too," Mary said, "even though I've never met them."

"Everyone likes Dickon. I wonder what he'd think of you."

"He wouldn't like me," said Mary sadly. "Nobody does."

"Do you like yourself?" Martha asked.

"Not really," replied Mary. "I never thought of that before."

As Martha headed home in high spirits, Mary felt lonelier than ever. She went outside and ran around the flower garden ten times. This made her feel much better. Wandering into the kitchen vegetable garden, she found Ben Weatherstaff.

"Springtime's coming," Ben said. "You can smell it in the soil."

Mary sniffed. The soil smelled nice and fresh and damp. "What kind of things will grow?" she asked.

"Oh, crocuses and snowdrops and daffodils."

Just then the robin fluttered down and landed close to Mary's feet. "Are any plants poking through in the robin's garden?" she asked.

Ben said gruffly, "I don't know anything about that garden and neither should you." Then he turned and walked away.

Mary shrugged and headed slowly down the path to the ivy-covered wall that had no door. Hearing a chirp and a twitter, she turned and saw that the robin had followed her.

17

Mary smiled. The robin was playing with her, pretending to peck for food. Mary made some robin sounds and crept slowly toward it. The robin let Mary get close. It liked her. This made Mary extremely happy.

She watched while the robin pecked and scratched at a hole in the ground. Mary thought she could see something rusty, like a brass ring, in the dirt. When the robin flew away, Mary rushed to the hole and pulled the rusty object out. It was an old key. "Hurray!" she shouted. "Maybe it's the key to the garden!"

With the key in her hand, Mary walked up and down the wall looking for a door. She looked hard but could not find one. Disappointed, she slipped the key into her pocket and decided to carry it with her whenever she went out. That way, she'd be ready if she ever did find the door.

The next day, Martha returned to Misselthwaite Manor in the best of spirits. "Everyone liked hearing about you," she said. "They wanted to hear all about India and the ship you came in."

"Did Dickon and your mother like to hear you talk about me?" asked Mary.

"Why, Dickon's eyes nearly popped out of his head, they got so round," replied Martha, smiling. "But Mother worried that you were alone too much. Look, " she said, pulling something from her apron, "I've brought you a present from my mother."

It was a jump rope, with a striped red-and-blue handle at each end. Mary had never seen one before, so Martha showed her how to skip with it. Mary was delighted and grateful. She knew Martha's mother did not have much money to buy such gifts.

The jump rope was a wonderful thing. Mary skipped rope down to the fountain garden, then up one walk and down another. At last she skipped into the kitchen garden and saw Ben Weatherstaff and the robin.

"Upon my word!" exclaimed Ben. "Jumping rope like a sweet child. Maybe you're not made of sour buttermilk, after all. What pink cheeks it's given you!"

Mary liked hearing this, and Ben encouraged her to keep on skipping. Soon, she went to her own special path to see if she could skip down it the whole way. Halfway down, Mary stopped to catch her breath. She saw the robin swaying on a long branch of ivy. The bird greeted her with a chirp. As Mary skipped toward it, she could feel the brass key strike against her pocket.

"You found the key for me yesterday," she said to the robin. "I wish you could show me the door today, but I don't think you know how!"

Just then, something happened that Mary would always say was magic. A gust of wind parted the trailing sprays of ivy hanging from the wall. It was then that Mary saw a round object—a doorknob! Mary's heart began to pound, and her hands shook as she pulled back the ivy and took out the brass key she always carried in her pocket.

She put the key into the lock and turned it. It took two hands to do it, but she finally turned the knob. Making sure no one was coming, she held back the swinging curtains of ivy and pushed back the door. It opened slowly. Then she slipped through the door and shut it behind her.

There she was, standing *inside* the secret garden. It was the sweetest, strangest-looking place anyone could imagine. The high walls were thickly matted with the leafless stems of climbing roses. The ground was covered with wintry brown grass and out of it grew clumps of bushes, possibly rosebushes, Mary thought. There were trees in the garden too. Climbing roses had run all over them, though Mary did not know if the roses were dead or alive. A hazy mantle of gray and brown branches spread over everything—walls, and trees, and even the brown grass. It all looked so mysterious.

"How still it is!" Mary whispered to the robin perched in one of the trees. "But no wonder. I'm the first person here in ten years."

She moved softly away from the door. Mary was glad that her steps made no sound, preserving the quiet. I hope the garden isn't completely dead, Mary thought, seeing no sign of leaves or buds anywhere. With her jump rope, Mary began to skip around the garden. Suddenly, she stopped and knelt down. In an alcove, she saw what once must have been a flowerbed, and she saw some little flower sprouts pushing up through the soil.

Remembering what Ben Weatherstaff had said, Mary thought the sprouts might be crocuses or snowdrops or daffodils. Slowly, she walked around the garden and looked for more sprouts. Finding many more, Mary became excited again.

"It isn't a dead garden!" she cried out softly to herself. "Even if the roses are dead, other things are alive!"

Mary did not know anything about gardening. But she noticed that some of the flower sprouts might not have enough room to grow because of the thick grass around them. Mary knelt down and, with a sharp piece of wood, dug and weeded until she cleared some space around them.

After she finished with the first flowerbeds, Mary went to the others, clearing the way for more sprouts and smiling the whole time without knowing it. The hours passed quickly before Mary realized she was late for her mid-day meal. "I'll come back this afternoon," she said, speaking to the trees and the rosebushes as if they heard her. Then she ran lightly across the grass, pushed open the old door and slipped through it under the ivy.

That noon, Mary ate a large dinner. Martha watched with

pleasure, wondering what brought on Mary's sudden appetite. Mary wanted to share her new secret with Martha. But Mary was afraid if Mr. Craven found out, he would get a new key and lock up the garden for good—something that Mary could not bear!

Instead, Mary said, "If Ben Weatherstaff would give me some seeds and lend me a small spade, I could make a little garden for myself."

"That's a lovely idea!" said Martha. "Dickon knows which flowers are the prettiest and how to make them grow. We could send him a letter and ask him to bring some garden tools and seeds." For the rest of the afternoon, Martha told Mary what to write in their letter to Dickon. Mary wrote it all down and then mailed the letter.

The sun shone down for nearly a week on the secret garden, the name Mary had given it. She liked the name and the beautiful walls that surrounded it. Best of all, she liked feeling she was in her own private world that no one else knew about.

Mary loved to garden, and the plants seemed to know how much she cared about them. With the grass cleared away, the sun could warm the flowers and the rain would be able to reach them at once. The plants began to feel very much alive.

Mary also liked talking with Ben Weatherstaff because he seemed to know everything about gardening. Ben himself seemed to enjoy talking with Mary, for she had stopped speaking to him as if he were a servant.

"The fresh air is doing you good," he said one day. "You're a bit healthier and not so pale. The first time I saw you, you looked like a young plucked crow."

"I know I'm heavier," said Mary. "My stockings don't wrinkle anymore."

Though Ben still got angry when she asked him about the walled-in garden, Mary liked him anyway.

One afternoon, Mary skipped down a path that led to a wooded park. At the park gate, she heard a low, peculiar whistling sound. Walking through the gate, she saw a boy sitting under a tree. He was playing a wooden pipe. The boy had a turned-up nose and the bluest eyes Mary had ever seen. A brown squirrel watched him from the tree, a cock pheasant peeked out from the bushes, and two rabbits sat up and sniffed. It actually seemed as if they were drawing near to listen to the boy's music.

When he saw Mary, the boy stopped his music and rose slowly. He didn't want to frighten the animals. "I'm Dickon," he said, "and I know you're Mary." He had a wide, curving mouth, and his smile brightened his entire face. Mary knew nothing about boys and felt rather shy, but Dickon did not seem to notice. He had received Martha's letter and had come with the garden tools and flower seeds they had requested. Excited, Mary asked to see the seeds.

"I've got a lot of mignonette and poppy seeds," Dickon said. "Mignonette's the sweetest-smelling thing that grows. It'll grow wherever you plant it, just like poppies." Dickon spoke quickly and easily. Mary liked him right off, and she soon forgot her shyness. "I'll plant the seeds for you myself," Dickon continued. "Where's your garden?"

Mary was not sure what to say. At last, clutching his sleeve, she asked, "Can you keep a secret?"

"Of course," he said. "If I couldn't keep secrets about such things as foxes' cubs and birds' nests, there'd be nothing safe on the moor."

Mary thought about this, but sharing her precious secret made her nervous.

"I've stolen a garden," she said. "But I'm the only one in the world who wants it to be alive."

Mary saw the puzzled look on Dickon's face. "Come , I'll show you," she said. Mary led Dickon to the wall, lifted the hanging ivy, and slowly pushed the door open. They entered together, and Mary waved her hand around proudly. "It's this," she said. "Have you heard of the secret garden?"

Dickon nodded, as he looked at the lovely tangle of trees and bushes. "What an odd, pretty place!" he said.

Dickon knew how to tell the dead branches from the live ones, and soon he was busy at work. He cut away the dead ones with his knife. Then he spotted Mary's own clearings around the flower sprouts. "Why, I thought you didn't know anything about gardening!" he exclaimed. "A gardener couldn't have taught you better."

Mary showed him more clearings, which Dickon said were full of crocuses, snowdrops, narcissuses, and daffodils. A chirp came from one of the trees. "Who's that robin calling?" he asked.

"Ben Weatherstaff," said Mary. "But it knows me too."

Dickon moved closer to the tree and made a sound almost like the robin's twitter. When the robin answered, Dickon said, "Yes, the bird's a friend of yours."

Mary thought Dickon was just as nice as she'd imagined he would be. And he could talk to birds and animals too! "You're the fourth person I like," she confessed to Dickon. The other three were Martha, Martha's mother, and Ben Weatherstaff. And there was also the robin, of course.

Later that same day, Mary rushed through her noon meal to get back to Dickon and the garden. Martha stopped her, however. "Mrs. Medlock says Mr. Craven wants to see you," she said. "He's going away for a long time to travel in foreign places, and he wants to meet you first."

Martha helped Mary into her best dress and brushed her hair. By the time Mary followed Mrs. Medlock down the long hallways to Mr. Craven's study, she was very nervous. Although she had been at Misselthwaite Manor for several weeks, Mary had never met her mysterious uncle. All she knew about him was that he had a crooked back and had acted strangely ever since his wife died. He must be some kind of monster! she thought, knocking on the study door.

"Come in!" Mr. Craven said. Mary entered and moved slowly toward him.

He's not too frightening, she thought to herself. He's just a man with high, crooked shoulders, and black hair streaked with white. If he didn't look so miserable, he might even be handsome. Still, Mary felt a little scared.

"Come here," Mr. Craven said. Mary stepped closer.

"What do you do here at Misselthwaite?" he asked.

"I play outdoors," gasped Mary. "I skip and run—and I look at the flower sprouts sticking up out of the earth."

"Don't look so scared," he said. "A child like you could not do any harm. What do you want—toys, books, dolls?"

Mary shook her head. "Could I have a bit of earth to plant seeds in?"

Mr. Craven studied Mary and answered slowly, "You remind me of someone else who loved the earth and things that grow. Take as much as you want that's not being used and make it come alive."

Mary was relieved. Now she could call the secret garden her own! She politely curtsied and left the study.

That night, Mary awoke to the rain beating against her window and the wind blowing around the corners and chimneys of the old house. She lay awake for some time, listening to the wind. It sounded to her like someone crying out on the moor.

Suddenly, something made her sit up and listen. "That isn't the wind," she whispered. "It's that crying I heard before!" Determined to find out what it was, Mary took the candle by her bedside and crept down the corridor. Soon she saw a glimmer of light beneath a door. The crying she heard was coming from that room.

Mary pushed the door open slowly, not knowing what to expect. Before her, on a carved, four-poster bed, was a boy crying fretfully. He had a sharp, delicate face and gray eyes. His thick hair tumbled over his forehead and made his face seem even smaller.

Seeing Mary's candlelight, he turned and stared. "Are you a ghost?" he asked in a frightened whisper.

Mary half-wondered if *he* might be a ghost, but she whispered back, "No, I'm Mary Lennox. Mr. Craven is my uncle."

"Oh. I'm his son, Colin," said the boy, no longer whispering or afraid.

"No one ever told me he had a son!" Mary exclaimed.

"They wouldn't dare. I don't like people to talk about me."

"Why?" asked Mary, feeling more curious every moment.

"Because I am always ill like this. If I live, I may have a crooked back, like my father's. But I won't live."

"What a strange house this is!" Mary said. "Everything is so secret. Have you been locked up?"

"No," said Colin. "I stay in this room because it would tire me to move out."

"Does your father come to see you?" asked Mary.

"Sometimes, but mostly when I'm asleep. My mother died when I was born, and I've heard people say it makes him miserable to look at me. He thinks I don't know, but I've heard people talking. He almost hates me."

"Do you ever go outside?" Mary asked.

"No," he said. "I hate people looking at me."

"In that case, shall I go away?"

"No," said Colin. "I want you to stay and talk with me."

Mary was glad. She wanted to know more about this mysterious boy. And Colin wanted to know all about her—when she had come to Misselthwaite, where her room was, and where she had lived before. Mary learned from Colin that he always got everything he wanted and never had to do anything he did not want to do. Mary realized she had been that way herself.

"I won't live long anyway," said Colin. He spoke as if the idea of dying had ceased to matter to him. "How old are you?" he asked suddenly.

"Ten. And so are you," said Mary, immediately wishing she had not said that.

"How do you know how old I am?" Colin demanded.

Mary clutched her hands nervously and said, "Because you were born when the garden was locked, ten years ago."

Now Colin wanted to know more about the garden, so Mary told him how it had come to be locked. She did not tell him she had found the key or that she had gone inside. It was too early to trust him with that.

Colin loved hearing about the garden. "I'll make the servants take me there and I'll let you go too," he said.

"Oh, no!" Mary cried.

"But you said you wanted to see it."

"I do," she said, "but we must keep it a secret for now!" Mary was terrified Colin would tell about the garden. If that happened, Dickon might not come back, the robin might fly away, and everything would be spoiled!

"If we keep the garden a secret and get into it someday," Mary said, "we could plant daffodils and lilies and snowdrops and watch them grow bigger every day. No one would know about it but us! Don't you think that would be wonderful?"

"I've never had a secret," Colin said, smiling. "But I'd like that."

The next day, Mary told Martha that she had met Colin. This upset the maid terribly. Martha was afraid she would be blamed for telling Mary. But Mary said that Colin was glad he had met her and wanted to see her every day. Mary then asked Martha if Colin really had a crooked back.

"Nobody knows for sure," said Martha. "Mr. Craven went crazy when he was born because Mrs. Craven had just died. He wouldn't set eyes on the baby. Mr. Craven said that it would have a crooked back like his and that it would be better off dead."

"But Colin doesn't look like he has a crooked back," said Mary.

"Not yet, but he began all wrong. The doctors said his back is weak, so they've always kept him lying down. They don't let him walk."

Mary thought a moment. "It's done me a lot of good to be outside," she said. "Do you think it would help Colin?"

"Oh, I don't know," replied Martha. "He was taken outside once and had such a fit of bad temper. He cried and cried, and made himself ill all night. Afterward, he said he never wanted to go outside again."

"He's a very spoiled boy," said Mary. "If he ever gets angry with me, I won't go see him again."

That afternoon, Colin ordered Martha to bring Mary to him. Poor Martha was shaking in her shoes when she brought Mary to the room. "I'm afraid Mrs. Medlock will think I told Mary about you," she said to Colin.

The boy frowned. "If I order you to bring Mary to me, that's your duty," he said. "Medlock has to do what I please, just as you do. Now, you may go."

After Martha left, Mary said to Colin, "You remind me of a little Indian prince, the way you order everyone around! You're so different from Dickon!"

"Who's Dickon?" Colin asked.

"He's Martha's brother," she said, "and he's not like anyone else in the world. He can charm foxes and squirrels and birds on the moor. When he plays his pipe, they come and listen."

"I couldn't go to the moor," Colin said. "I'm going to die." It was almost as if Colin were boasting about it.

"See here," said Mary crossly, "let's not talk about dying. Let's talk about living. Let's start by talking about Dickon." And that's what they did. They enjoyed themselves so much that they forgot about the time. For a while, Colin even forgot about his back.

It rained for a week. So there had been no chance to see the secret garden or Dickon. But Mary enjoyed herself by spending many hours each day with Colin in his room. They often looked at beautiful books and pictures, and they took turns reading to each other. They laughed about silly things, and Colin liked to talk about the secret garden and what might be in it.

In their talks, Mary tried to find out if Colin could really be trusted not to tell about the garden. If he could, she had to think of a way to get him there without anyone finding out.

Finally, the rain stopped one morning and the sun returned. Sunshine poured through the blinds. Mary jumped out of bed and ran to open the window. The sky was blue again, and fresh, cool air blew in. No one else was awake yet, but Mary could not wait to see her garden.

Once inside the secret walls, Mary was surprised to see Dickon already there. "I couldn't stay in bed!" he exclaimed. "When the sun jumped up, I ran all the way here."

The rain and warmth had pushed the crocuses up into whole clumps of purple and orange and gold. Leaf buds were bursting on the rose branches that had once seemed dead. Mary and Dickon found so many more wonders that they kept forgetting to keep their voices low. Best of all, Mary thought, was seeing Ben Weatherstaff's robin building a nest in the garden.

"He'll get nervous if we watch too closely," warned Dickon.

To take their minds off the robin, Mary told Dickon about Colin. "He always thinks about how a lump's going to form on his back," she said.

Dickon shook his head. "If we could get him out here, he wouldn't be watching for lumps to grow on his back. He'd be watching for buds to grow on the rosebushes."

"I've been thinking that too," said Mary. "If he could keep a secret, maybe you could push his wheelchair out here without anyone seeing us."

"I'm sure the garden in springtime would be better than doctor's stuff for Colin," said Dickon.

Mary spent the whole delightful day in the garden with Dickon. But that evening, Martha stood at her door with a worried face. "I wish you'd gone to see Colin today," she said. "He was nearly having a fit!"

Colin was still in a rage when Mary went to see him. "I won't let that boy come here if you go and play with him instead of me," he said.

This made Mary angry. "Then I'll never come into this room again!"

"I'll make you," said Colin. "They'll drag you in."

"That they may," said Mary fiercely. "But I'll just sit here and clench my teeth and never tell you one thing."

"You are so selfish!" cried Colin.

"You're more selfish than I am," said Mary. "You're the most selfish boy I ever saw."

"That's not true!" Colin shouted. "Besides, I'm going to die!"

"I don't believe it," said Mary firmly. "You just say that to make people feel sorry for you." With that, Colin picked up his pillow and threw it at her. Furious, Mary walked to the door, then turned. "I was going to tell you about Dickon and his fox and crow," Mary said, her face pinched tight. "But now I won't." She marched out the door and closed it behind her.

Back in her room, Mary found Martha waiting for her with a box that Mr. Craven had sent. Though Mary had felt cross after her fight with Colin, her anger melted when she saw the beautiful books that her uncle had sent. Two were about gardening. She had never expected him to remember her and wanted to thank him immediately.

As she wrote a letter to Mr. Craven, she thought of Colin. Normally, she would be sharing these new treasures with him. She remembered how Colin thought about his back most when he'd been cross or tired, which he certainly had been today. "I'll go see him tomorrow," Mary decided.

In the middle of the night, Mary was awakened by such dreadful sounds that she jumped out of bed in an instant. "It's Colin!" she said to herself. He was sobbing and screaming at the top of his lungs. "Somebody must stop him!" she said angrily. "He'll upset everyone in the house!"

Her temper mounted as she flew down the corridor and into Colin's room. "Stop it!" she shouted. "You'll scream yourself to death!"

Colin looked dreadful, all pale and swollen, and he was gasping and choking. But Mary did not seem to care.

"If you scream," she said, "I'll scream, too. And I can scream louder!"

"I can't stop! I felt the lump on my back and now I shall die!" Colin wept.

"There's nothing the matter with your stupid back," said Mary. "Sobbing and screaming make lumps. Turn over and let me look at it." Mary looked carefully at Colin's thin back. "There's no lump," she announced. "And if you ever say there's a lump there again, I'll laugh!"

"Do you think . . . I could . . . live to grow up?" he said.

"You probably could if you'd stop having these fits of anger and spend some time outside every day," said Mary.

Colin was relieved. He was weak with crying, but his temper tantrum had passed. He put his hand out toward Mary.

"I'll . . . I'll go outdoors with you, Mary," he said. Mary sat by his bed and described how the coming of spring had changed the garden. Her voice was soft, and Colin slowly relaxed until he was fast asleep. Then Mary quietly returned to her own room and slept.

Up with the morning sun, Mary dressed quickly and went out to the secret garden. Dickon was already there. He was surrounded by the two squirrels he called Nut and Shell and by the crow he named Soot. When she told him what happened the night before, he said, "Yup! We've got to get him out here quick!"

Just then Nut scampered up onto Dickon's shoulder, causing his cap to fall on Nut's head. The two burst out laughing. "I'll tell Colin what your clever pet did today!" Mary said.

"That'll make him laugh," agreed Dickon. "And there's nothing as good as laughing for sick folks."

When Mary visited Colin that morning, he exclaimed, "You smell like flowers—and fresh things!"

"It comes from sitting on the grass and watching a squirrel called Nut knock Dickon's cap off his head and onto its own!" Mary said, laughing.

Colin began to laugh as she told him what happened. Pretty soon, the two of them could not stop themselves from laughing. When they could speak again, Colin told Mary he did not mean what he said about sending Dickon away.

"I'm glad you said that," said Mary, ready to burst with the news of the garden. "He's coming to see you tomorrow with his animal friends." Colin was delighted.

"But that's not all," Mary said. "There's a door to the garden. I found it and went inside weeks ago. But I couldn't tell you until I was sure I could trust you."

Colin was cheerful and wide awake when Mary came in the next morning. At breakfast, he said to Mrs. Medlock in his most prince-like manner, "A boy and a fox, a crow, two squirrels, and a newborn lamb are coming to see me today. I want them brought up as soon as they arrive."

Mrs. Medlock gasped. "Yes, sir," she said.

Mary and Colin had just finished eating when Mary said, "Listen! Did you hear a caw? That must be Soot!"

Dickon's boots went *clump, clump, clump* as he walked down the hall. He entered the room smiling broadly with the newborn lamb in his arms and the fox trotting by his side. Soot sat on one shoulder, Nut trailed behind, and Shell's head poked out of Dickon's coat pocket.

Colin stared in wonder, but Dickon did not mind. He put the newborn lamb in Colin's lap and gave him a bottle to feed it. Dickon, Colin and Mary talked about animals and about the garden, which Dickon and Mary said had a new patch of flowers.

A week of cold, windy weather passed before Mary and Dickon were able to take Colin out. During this time, the three children discussed over and over just how they were going to get Colin to the garden without Mrs. Medlock or the servants seeing them.

When the day finally came, the strongest footman in the house carried Colin into a wheelchair waiting outside. The footman was then promptly excused. Dickon pushed the wheelchair slowly and steadily, while Mary walked beside it. Colin leaned back and looked at the bright sky. Not another human creature was to be found on the paths they took. Even so, as they approached the ivy-covered wall, they began to speak in excited whispers.

"Here's the handle and here's the door," Mary said. "Push him in quickly, Dickon!" And Dickon did it with one strong push.

Inside, Colin looked around at all the leaves and splashes of color and the trees with birds twittering in them. A pink glow of color crept into his face.

"I shall get well!" Colin cried out. "I shall live forever and ever and ever!"

From his chair, placed beneath the plum tree's snow-white blossoms, Colin watched as Mary and Dickon worked around the garden. Sometimes they all got to talking and giggling so loudly that they had to put their hands over their mouths. Colin had been told about the law of whispers and low voices, and he liked the secrecy of it.

"I don't want this afternoon to end," Colin said. "But I'll come back tomorrow and all the days after that."

"You certainly will," said Dickon, "and we'll have you walking about here like other people before long."

"Walk!" exclaimed Colin, turning bright red. "Do you think I will?"

Just then Colin looked up at the wall. "Who's that man?" he asked in a loud whisper. Mary and Dickon looked up, scrambling to their feet.

Ben Weatherstaff glared at them from the top of a ladder behind the wall. He shook his fist at Mary and shouted, "You nosy girl, always poking about where you aren't wanted!"

"But the robin showed me the way," Mary protested.

"Do you know who I am?" Colin demanded.

Ben Weatherstaff stared and answered at last in a shaky voice, "Yes, yes, I do—with your mother's eyes staring at me out of your face. You're the boy with the crooked back."

"I do not have a crooked back!" Colin shouted.

Ben did not know what to say. "Y—you mean you don't even have crooked legs?"

Now the strength that usually threw Colin into a fit of anger rushed through him in a new way. In a moment, he was filled with a power he had never known. He began to throw off his blankets, and Dickon rushed to help him. Suddenly, Colin's thin legs pushed out from the wheelchair and his feet touched the grass.

"Come on, you can do it!" whispered Mary.

And in a moment Colin was standing upright.

Ben Weatherstaff forgot his anger, then tears ran down his cheeks. "Why, the lies people tell!" he exclaimed. "You'll be a man yet. And a healthy one at that!"

Colin stood straighter and straighter as he spoke. "I want to talk to you," he said to Ben, gesturing for him to come down to the garden. "Now that you've seen us, you'll have to be in on the secret. What work do you do in the gardens, Ben?" he asked.

"Anything I'm told to do," replied the gardener. "I'm kept on by favor. You see, your mother liked me."

"Was this her garden?" asked Colin, surprised.

"Yes, and she was very fond of it."

Colin told Ben that he could help in the garden as long as he kept it a secret. Ben surprised all of them when he said, "After your mother died, I came here once a year until I got too old to climb over the wall. I did a bit of pruning, for your mother once said to me, 'Ben, if I ever go away, you must take care of my roses'."

Colin, Mary, and Dickon saw that they could trust Ben. After a while, Ben said to Colin, "How'd you like to plant a rose I have in a pot?"

Colin was thrilled. "Just think! Not only have I stood up for the first time today, but now I'm also going to dig!"

Dickon and Mary helped Colin dig the hole for the rose. His face flushed as he set the rose in the mold. Ben then filled the hole with earth and packed it down firmly.

As the strange, lovely afternoon ended, Dickon helped Colin to his feet. Colin stood up and, looking into the setting sun, laughed as he had never laughed before.

That evening, Colin said to Mary, "I'm not going to be a poor sick thing anymore. I stood on my feet this afternoon." Colin and Mary believed there was good magic—or *something*—in the garden that made the flowers bloom and made them strong and healthy. And in the happy months that followed, it did seem the garden worked magic.

Colin spent every day in the garden, even gray days. He would lie on the grass watching the insects, plants, and birds with equal fascination. If the magic in the garden made things grow, he thought it had also gotten him to stand.

One day, Colin said to Mary, Dickon, and Ben: "When I was going to try to stand that first time, I remember Mary whispering to me, 'You can do it!' And I did. Now I am going to walk around the whole garden!"

Colin rose slowly, with Mary and Dickon on either side. Ben Weatherstaff walked behind and the lamb, fox cub, Soot, and a white rabbit trailed after them. The procession moved slowly, stopping every few yards to rest, until Colin had walked all the way around the garden.

"I did it!" he cried. "This is to be the biggest secret of all. No one will know anything about it until I can walk and run like any boy." Most of all, Colin wanted to surprise his father when he returned home from his trip abroad.

During the time Colin was discovering the joys of the secret garden, his father was walking through a quiet forest in Austria. Archibald Craven had traveled throughout Europe, seeing some of the most beautiful places in the world. But their beauty did not seem to touch him.

In the silence of the Austrian forest, Mr. Craven decided to rest for a while. He lay down on a carpet of moss next to a stream. Soon he fell into a deep, deep sleep. When he awoke, he shook his head in wonder.

"What a strange, wonderful dream I had!" he exclaimed. "There was Colin, clear as day, crying out, 'I am going to live forever and ever and ever!'"

Mr. Craven was puzzled by the dream, but did not think much more about it. Still, as he continued traveling, Mr. Craven slowly felt stronger and happier. He slept well at

night. And when he looked in the mirror, his back no longer seemed so crooked.

Gradually, he began to think of Misselthwaite Manor. One night, he dreamed he was in his wife's garden. The dream seemed so real that he thought he smelled the roses. A few days later, Mr. Craven decided to go home.

As the train whirled him through mountain passes and grassy plains, Mr. Craven thought about his son. He had not meant to be a bad father, but he had never really felt like a father at all. Now that he felt so much better, Mr. Craven looked at his life in a new way.

Perhaps I have been wrong all these years, he thought. Suddenly, he wanted very much to see the son he had neglected for so long.

When he arrived back home at last, Mr. Craven asked, "Where is Colin?"

"In the garden, sir," replied Mrs. Medlock.

Mr. Craven went immediately to the ivy-covered door. Then he stopped and listened. There were sounds inside the garden—sounds of running, scuffling feet, exclamations, and happy cries. As he listened, the sounds grew louder and louder. Curious, he yanked the door wide open.

At that moment a boy burst through the door and dashed headlong into him. Caught by surprise, Mr. Craven held out his arms just in time to save the boy from falling.

This was not the meeting Colin had planned. "Father!" he said, standing as tall as he could. "It's me, Colin."

Mr. Craven could scarcely believe his eyes.

"No one knows I can walk," his son continued breathlessly. "We kept it a secret so you would be the first to know. I'm well, and I just beat Mary in a footrace. I'm going to be an athlete!"

He said it all like a healthy boy—his face flushed, his words tumbling over each other in eagerness. Mr. Craven shook with joy as he embraced his son. For the rest of the day, Mary, Dickon, and Colin took turns telling him about the garden and its magic.

As the sun set that day, Martha and Mrs. Medlock looked out toward the garden. They could hardly believe their eyes. Walking along one side of Mr. Craven were Mary and Dickon and a parade of little animals. On the other side, Mr. Craven had his arm around his son's shoulders. He was beaming. And Colin, feeling stronger than ever, proudly walked beside him. It was the first of what would be many walks together.

	DATE DUE		

F   Burnett, Frances
BUR   Hodgson
            The secret garden